I0782120

Shattered
Reflections
Of
An
Unforgiveable
Love

TABLE OF CONTENTS

>>>>>>>>THE BEGINNING >>>>>>>

Standing in the bedroom doorway, I am perplexed as I watch him sleeping, seemingly comfortably. How can he sleep at this time? I have not slept all night and my head and heart ache with pain. How can he sleep at a time like this? My head hurts from the constant thought of "what can I do?" And my heart aches from the harsh words that were spoken. How can he sleep at such a time? I stand with tears streaming, then quietly walk to the kitchen to make a cup of tea.

As the kettle sounds for tea time, he awakens. I am frozen with fear, pain and confusion. My thoughts are racing--"YOU MUST DO SOMETHING TO REPAIR THE DAMAGE, DO SOMETHING TO MAKE IT RIGHT, DO SOMETHING!"

He is in the bathroom preparing for the start of his new day. I take a seat in the front of the bay window while sipping on my tea, hoping the sun and clear skies will guide me. Quietly and patiently I await and finally he emerges. Complete with a newly purchased ensemble for the start of his new day, he approaches me with a different stride in his steps.

Engulfed with fear but realizing this is my time to make things right, I rise slowly and walk toward him. I extend my arm to rest my hand on his chest. He offers a silent, nonchalant observation. I inhale and with tears in my eyes these words are spoken: "Please do not do this. I will do all that I can to make you happy." He starts to speak—I stop him.

"Please let me just say this. I will do better, I will cook and clean better, I will fulfill any sexual desires that you have, I will do anything you ask of me. I do not think I can love you any more than I do but I will love better catering to your every desire. I WILL BE BETTER—just please do not do this to us—I love you."

He pulls my hand away as I try to hold onto him. He turns away, and with his back turned walking out of the house, his final words to me are, "I DO NOT LOVE YOU ANY LONGER. I LOVE HER AND YOU NEED TO BE OUT OF MY HOUSE TODAY!"

I awaken to sunrise. My eyes heavily and slowly open to surroundings that I no longer yearn. I am still in this moment of bewilderment, despair and anger. I hear activity—life's purpose, life's determination, life's motivation and lastly life's language—none of which I desire. I am motionless—looking at the bedroom ceiling with scrambled and hopeless thoughts. Although my thoughts are not suicidal, the desire to live is too burdensome. At this moment I only have one aspiration to experience "eternal sleep."

TIME WAITS FOR NO MAN OR WOMAN

FORWARD SIX MONTHS

Awakening, once again, I stare at the ceiling, hoping this day will provide motivation. In the distance I hear voices, visualize faces and smell breakfast being prepared. I lie in bed and reflect on all things. My thoughts are fast and furious—I want to live but am lifeless. I want to progress but I am too fragile. I want to travel toward the light but I can see only the dismal darkness of my existence. I wish to vibrantly inhale the gift of life and love. Possibly, I am not worthy, warranted or equipped to receive these possessions. In this moment of despair, my eyes close and I silently weep. In this moment of misery I welcome endless sleep.

Several hours later I am awakened with a gesture of life and love. My best friend enters my sanctuary with a dinner plate--salad, shrimp scampi, rice, garlic bread and a glass of red wine—no less served on a tray with two gorgeous roses in a crystal vase. She places the tray on a bedside table and softly speaks the words, "we love you, and we want and need you. Please do not die but take all the time you need to cry, Then Try! Love You C." She slowly walks to the bedroom exit, stands in the doorway and softly speaks the words, "Those roses are pretty and they need water, Love You C." The door closes.

I uncover my head and wipe my tears. I rise from the bed, walk to the mirror and look into my eyes—desolation is the reflection. I walk to the table and look at the simplicity of this "love" made tray and think those roses are pretty. There were two roses—one blue and the other black. I thought--Yes, they are pretty and need watering to grow and at this moment nourishment is what I need. I began to devour the dinner served by my best friend, Stephanie, who was a sterling cook. Sipping on the large

glass of red wine, my mental and internal wave shifted. I
wanted to grasp it but sleep overwhelmed the moment.

HOLD ON^^^^HOLD ON^^^^HOLD ON BABY

IF YOU SURVIVE THE DARKNESS IN THE NIGHT

TOMORROW MORNING LIGHT ALWAYS ARRIVES

It has been approximately 10 months.   I have reflected, revisited regrets, and remembered the innocent sweetness.   Now I am rejoicing in surviving this unwarranted and unforeseen heartbreak.

It was as if I were a toddler taking steps for the first time. I uncovered my seemingly lifeless body and rose to the task of living and rebuilding myself. Slowly walking to the window, opening the blinds, I smile. Slowly walking to the bedroom and exiting the door, I smile. I am determined to be better than I was yesterday and all of the yesteryears.

Reflection is always 20/20 hindsight. I should have begun healing my mental state and the physical would align. One achieves most results when one's "mind is right." I would come to realize that heartbreak is heartache and it seems only to the one who aches that this is a forever experience one could endure. There will be much personal pain, anguish and despair that will seemingly make this heartache mild in comparison.

Phone ringing—6:00 AM.

"Hey, Girl."

"Hey, good morning what's up?"

"Are you going this morning?"

"Yep, will be ready at 6:30."

"Ok, cool. I will meet you at the park."

"Alright, see you there."

My name is Crystal Chandelier Tyson. The story goes my mom admired crystal chandeliers of all styles. For some reason I never felt connected to the name, so all called me "CC" or "C."

I began my quest for physical and mental wellness after I survived that tumultuous heartbreak and heartache. My workout routine is 2 hours 3 days per week. Often my girlfriend Stephanie meets me at the park for an outdoor workout. We would exercise, jog and at the end of the routine, we would cool down for about 30 minutes. The cool down is the most enjoyable part, because we talk and laugh about things.

On this particular summer day we spent several hours at the park—enjoying people watching and conversing with one another. The day was early and we decided to return home for household chores and then take the evening to hang out. It is the Earth, Wind & Fire concert tonight—Stephanie would get the tickets. It had been almost a year that I entered a club or enjoyed a concert. Needless to say, I was ready to step out and have some fun. I had no expectations for the night, only to "INHALE AND EXHALE" with drinks, laughter and dance.

The evening started with the concert—EWF—which put me in a frenzied state of mind. Simply EWF concert was "off the chain." We had a good time.

Afterward, we decided to do the "club scene." I considered this my coming out moment. I had reflected, revised and immensely improved my physical and mental state. It seemed as though I was in a cocoon waiting for my moment to arrive. I was not seeking commitment or a love interest. Actually, I only desired to dance, drink and think (and in that order).

Our first club was a nice pick, the crowd was not too belligerent and it was standing room only when we arrived. While ordering our drinks at the bar, there were two men sitting, and they offered us their seats. They did not appear to be overbearing or obnoxious—they were merely courteous toward two ladies.

Stephanie ordered the first round. Previously, I had not been a drinker of alcohol. Once she ordered she wanted to make a proclamation—once the drinks arrived---she swiveled in her stool, looked at me, gently held my face in her hands and with a loving and concerned tone she said. "Sister Love, I do not know all that went wrong with you and that asshole and I do not need to know everything. What I do know and what I need you to accept, recognize and acknowledge is that you are an exceptional, giving and loving woman. You did not hesitate to put him before you. You dreamt his dream when he stopped dreaming. You energized him to reinvigorate his career. Although, he did not have to get on bended knee, he should have been obliged not to betray or do you wrong. You survived the disaster without defeat. CC, you rock and do not give another person 100% of your being---have a percentage in reserve when you may need it. I am overjoyed that you have arrived. "Welcome Back."

I heard her words and I did not respond. In my rational state of being I realized I did not make it happen for him but I did support and dedicate all my efforts to his vision for his career and life. Tonight was a good start for the beginning of the rest of my life. With each failure I overcame I thought the present pain is the worst. I had cried my last tear for the last time.

I wanted to dance, so we danced and drank for the entire night. With each dance it seemed as though I was shedding another layer of pain. It felt good and I needed this outing. We went for breakfast and returned home around 7:00am. (Don't stop get it, get it---we had fun).

IN THE MIDST OF IT ALL

I moved back home with the family and it was a nice fit. I was feeling better about my person, purpose and promise. All other siblings had left home, so it was my parents and me. My mornings were spent lying in bed sipping on tea and watching television until mid morning. At times I would exercise in the evenings because I wanted to intake the tranquility of the mornings. Both my parents were employed which provided me with my daily essentials and necessities. When I moved away I did not take any of my clothing or bedroom furnishings. I asked them to keep my room as it were because I would still come and spend time with them. They agreed and wished me happiness. I was not employed for a long while and they did not pressure me for a hasty decision.

Usually, I would clean house and cook dinner in the late morning or afternoon. I would make errand runs for my parents--paying bills, grocery shopping, etc. They were appreciative and enjoyed my presence which allowed me time and liberty.

This particular day, I decided to do three runs. I ran to the park, did my exercise routine at the park and ran home. I returned home to manage household chores and cook a good dinner. Stephanie invited me over to her house for ladies night card playing. I asked if we could make it for next weekend because I wanted to chill at home with my parents. She agreed only if I agreed to assist her with the cooking—I said cool, we will do it next Saturday.

My peeps (parents) arrived home later that evening. We sat around talking, laughing and loving each other. They told me life stories and lessons. Most were informative journeys of their lives and some were amusing. Several hours later I prepared their plates, sat and sipped on lemonade as they ate. I did not want to eat because I wanted to make my last run at the park. My peeps would talk about folk wisdom frequently. One they would express: "You will live and learn, and then you will learn to live." Dismal experiences will make you better or bitter depending on your understanding and perspective—hence you will learn. When I was younger and acted silly, to verbally scold me they would ask, "Are you a fool or a damn fool?" or "If you are going to be a fool, don't be a damn fool, Crystal." When I was permitted to answer the question my response would be:

"I'm not a fool."

"Then stop acting like a damn fool and go sit your silly acting ass down until you know better." (The sweet reflections of childhood and infantile innocence—how I wish for the days of ole.)

The atmosphere sitting with my peeps as they ate dinner was of unspoken UNCONDITIONAL LOVE that engulfed our presence. Unbeknownst to me I would never experience "that love" which I would always seek and desire. It was a pleasant and gratifying evening with my peeps. As I washed dinner dishes, I SMILED. It had been a while since I genuinely SMILED and felt the CELEBRATION of ME!

^^^^LIFE IS A THREE PART ACT: ^^^^

Part 1: The Beginning--Birth

Part 2: The Middle—Life

Part 3: The End--Death

PART 2 OF THIS THING CALLED LIFE

IN THE THICK OF THINGS

As I walked to the park for my late run, I began to have a different stride in my steps. As the summer breeze propelled me forward, I SMILED with the thought that I have ARRIVED! I was focused on "doing it different to get to something better." I SMILED.

I arrived at the park—it was active. This summertime boosts good personal energies. There were some couples sitting on benches, some walking and a couple of joggers. I began my stretching routine then began my run. My enhanced endurance made it possible for the completion of three entire park laps for the first time. I obtained a sensation of accomplishment. Completing my cooling down process I approached a bench to sit, taking time to relax and looking at the engaging scenery. Gazing at the beautiful evening stars, I detected a fragrance in the air and a man appeared. He stopped near the bench and was adjusting his walkman earphones. He began a singing, dancing and sprinting routine. Although noticeable, he was not disruptive. People were exchanging pleasantries with me as they passed. As he would pass with his impressive routine I would observe that it was his distinct fragrance in the air.

He did not invoke any erotic desire within me; I was not interested in any romantic involvement. Although I had been practicing celibacy, I still admired and respected the male species. I decided not to do anything that would jeopardize my journey of healing.

After an hour on the bench I decided to return home. Suddenly, he appeared with a slight limp and sat at the opposite end. It was visible that he was experiencing minor physical distress.

"Forgive me, I do not want to disturb you, but I must sit for a few seconds."

I asked "are you ok?"

"I fell during my last sprint."

"How did it occur?"

"I decided for my last sprint to run the upper level and the track was cracked." I repeated "the track was cracked." Laughter followed.

"I am embarrassed."

"No need for embarrassment, I'm sure you are a manly man when the tracks don't crack your ass." Laughter ensued.

"Oh, you got jokes. You're the old funny lady they told me about."

Several seconds of laughter followed.

It was getting late and I wanted to go home for dinner. With the next few seconds of silence, with the occasional passing of warm breezes, with the calm surroundings, with unpressured conversation and laughter, I closed my eyes and felt this is the right moment, I INHALED THEN EXHALED. I opened my eyes and at that moment our eyes connected. With shyness I looked away and in a voice that exuded strength, kindness, compassion, consideration and sexiness he stated "My name is Phoenix Washington and it has been my privilege to meet you, and I would like to know your name."

I looked at him and said "My name is Crystal and my friends call me CC."

He responded, "This has been a pleasant meeting and if allowed the opportunity, I'm sure it would be gratifying getting to know you so that I would become a friend to call you CC."

With my detection of him being a "take-charge man" our initial encounter was good. I did not expect anything because I was at peace with being alone and not lonely. As of yet, I had not become an anti-male bashing woman. I was not uncomfortable or compromised by his presence. With precaution, I chose to change the subject. We conversed and exchanged laughter for a while longer. It seemed we were proponents of laughter. Primarily due to my shyness, he took charge of the conversation. I heard some vitals and zoned out for others. (This is my modus operandi. A word will trigger a past experience or emotion and then my thoughts will mutely take me elsewhere. At times, as I heard his voice, I would smile. Periodically, I would look at him and realize that with his meticulous wording and swagger he was attracted to me. In another place and time I also was attracted in the abstract to him. Continuously, in traveled space I thought,   NOT NOW MY FRIEND, NOT NOW!

Listening to his "groove" I was in a calm and balanced position. We sat on the bench for hours and finally it was time to bid farewell. I mentioned that I was going home to eat dinner. He responded with an invitation.

"I cannot let you go without taking you somewhere to grab a bite to eat."

"That is not necessary at all. I need to go home because it is getting late."

"Are you sure? It would be a pleasure to share a salad with you. We should not eat excessively at this hour but you should eat. Besides, it is the least I can do."

Thought to Self He is a smooth operator. His demeanor is not at all offensive or intimidating. His words are very cordial and welcoming which make me feel at ease. It is now approaching 9:30ish and I am hungry. He interrupted my thought with, "Are you driving?"

"No, why do you ask?"

"I was going to suggest this decent eatery a few blocks from here and you could meet me there. If you are ill at ease with being my passenger, we could walk there it is about a 20 minute walk."

"Afterwards, I would still need to go home."

"Well, that is correct Miss Crystal, I will call you a taxi and you will arrive home safely."

"Can you walk a few blocks without pain?"

"I'm good to go now, just needed to rest my leg. The walk will do me good if you do not mind."

"I do not mind."

As we leisurely strolled, talked and laughed we became somewhat friendly with one another. At one point we crossed an intersection and he took hold of my hand. Arriving at the restaurant was a mixture of reserve and friendliness.

Once seated while looking at the menu, he tenderly took my menu and said, "I am going to ask that you let me order for us and I think you will enjoy my choosing. Have you ever been to this place?"

"No."

"Remember when I said it would be a delight to share a salad with you?"

"Yes, I wondered why you suggested we share a salad."

"Let me order for us--the salad of my choice and if you do not like it or the experience you do not have to see me again or give me your phone number."

"That's a challenge that will be rewarding."

"Oh, yeah you are the funny lady again." Laughter followed.

When the waitress arrived they exchanged familiar pleasantries. He instructed the kitchen to "do it royally with double ingredients."

This salad would be one that I had not heard of or seen before. They served us a variety of different salad dressings with "crystal" wine glasses and plates. I took a moment to admire the subtle romantic arrangement. *Self-Thought-- He is a take-charge guy that does it with such sleekness and smoothness.* As I gazed at the crystal, there was a sensation of good vibes for our first encounter. He interrupted my thought with

"What kind of dressing would you like?"

"Blue Cheese."

"I have yet to try a blend of dressings. Have you ever tried that?"

"I have not tried a blend and why do you want to try it?"

"Primarily because this has to be the best salad you have ever eaten so that I may have the opportunity to see you again. Secondly, it would be nice for us to experience a first time with one another. Your first taste will determine our future." We laughed and I said, "Ok, let's see what you got." He looked at me with a sexy smirk and said "Beware, you may be submerged with me in your future."

"Oh geez, then my future is not looking too promising."

Laughter, laughter and more laughter.

He responded, "You're always saying some funny slick things and I like it. I enjoy laughing because laughter is good for one."

"Yes, I agree, I like to laugh and have fun; I can tell you do also."

He looked at me in the eyes and said "That's one commonality for us, which would be a good future start."

He prepared my plate and added the dressing combo, poured us a glass of wine and stated, "On the count of three...our future will begin or cease to exist...."and the countdown began. As he was counting I began to recognize his attractiveness—he was a handsome and charming man. NOT NOW MY FRIEND—NOT NOW was seemingly more in the distance. It had been since my heartbreak that I was in the company of a man especially in this atmosphere. I heard the number three and we took a heaping fork full of salad with oily dressing dripping, he extended his napkin. "Do not speak Crystal, just eat." Laughter

We silently ate for several minutes. This salad is scrumptious, this man and his swag are appealing and this experience gratifying. Pondering his silence I finally spoke after 10 or so minutes.

"This salad is delicious." He continued to eat in silence. I spoke again.

"Yes, this has been a nice first greeting and I will probably order this salad again." Still he continued to eat in silence. At that moment the waitress appeared at the table and he asked her for pen and paper. He wrote something on it and passed it to me—it read: Now give up your digits. The thought of having you in my future is enticing. Our eyes met and at this point my defenses were weakening. As I nervously wrote my number and passed it, I said, "A bet is a bet. I guess my future could be worse." Laughter ensued. He stood, came over to me and kissed me on the cheek with a whisper in my ear. "Thank you. Your future was bright without me. Now it's gleaming with me. I'll be right back." I was relieved he left to give me some time with self. His kiss activated a sensitivity that I could not express but did not fail to entertain. I did not desire an intimate relationship—NOT NOW MY FRIEND···NOT NOW. I started to surmise that we can have association that will develop companionship. Deciding that all is suitable, I became undisturbed in my thoughts with this rendezvous and I smiled.

He returned, as he passed me, his hand delicately rubbed and nested on my back for a few seconds. His touch transmitted a reassurance of this delightful and pleasant time spent. He entertained me for a few hours, joking, laughing and exchanging some vitals. Finally, it was time for us to bid farewell. He asked the waitress to call a taxi for me and I thought, "Wow, this is true to form···he did not try to pressure me to go home with him or for him to take me home." The taxi arrived quickly and walking with me, he expressed that he enjoyed spending time with me and was looking forward to the next time. Opening the door he gave the driver $10 and said, "I do not know where she lives but if that is not enough just come back for the difference." I was astounded that the driver responded, "Ok, that's cool, Phoenix." He leaned into the window and I thought he was going to try and kiss me but to my disbelief he only said, "I will call you in about 30 minutes to make sure you made it home safely."

"How are you getting your vehicle from the park," I asked.

"Do not worry; I'll get it and call you again when I get home, ok?"

"Okay."

As the taxi drove me home, the quietness permitted me the opportunity to meditate. I relished in the delight of this evening with him and yearned for my pajamas and bed. Once home, I made me a bath and with the vapors, I disentangled all negativity and only enjoyable thoughts of tonight were cuddled. It seemed as if harmony surrounded that moment in time. I put on pajamas and went to my bedroom. I turned on the stereo and the "quiet storm" put me to sleep. Several hours later I awakened by the phone ringing.

"Hello."

"Hello is the Crystal."

Yes, would you hold?" I had to potty and get a drink. The mood was set for conversation.

"I'm back, how are you doing in these early hours?"

"Once Goldie returned from his trip taking you home, knowing that you were safe at home, I decided to stay at the restaurant and work."

"I noticed your familiarity with everyone including the taxi driver. I started to think you get around."

Laughingly, he said "Actually, it is my family owned restaurant/lounge and I am one of the co-managers."

"That explains the royal treatment."

"No, you received the red carpet. Next date will be the royal settings."

Laughter

It had been some time since I had received a man's exclusive attention. While I believed that I was not interested in a romantic relationship, as we conversed it was enchanting. Our conversation entailed the preliminary groundwork. We discussed interests, goals, family, lifestyles etc. Time passed and it was dawn before we had our finale. He would call again.

Rising in the mid morning I found my Mother cooking her famous French toast breakfast. She put on the teapot and we sat at the table. Sipping on tea as she ate, I wondered if she and my Dad were full of pride and content with me, or if somehow my failures filled them with disappointment and appeasement. We sat in stillness until she asked, "How was your run last evening?"

"It was good and interesting."

"You were out later than usual and I did hear the phone ring late."

"Yes, I met this guy at the park. While running, he injured his leg and we sat on the bench for a long while talking. When it became late he invited me to his restaurant for dinner."

"Oh, well I guess that was good and interesting." We laughed.

She rose majestically and with her wisdom acknowledging the sentiment, she hugged me and kissed my forehead. I kissed her cheek and said "I love you Mama." She started to clear the table and whispered, "Keep giving us flowers and roses as we are alive and I am certain I love you more." I laughed and said, "Yeah, Mom you probably do."

Later that day I called Stephanie and we planned our gathering for Saturday. We spoke about Phoenix and she was pleasantly surprised, stating, "Girl, it is your time to have fun and love. You deserve it."

"Yeah, but I am not on a love quest."

"I did not say only love, have fun initially and let the relationship take its course. Besides, most men are not looking for love so do not stress about the love quest." Laughter ensued.

It was Thursday and I decided to chill at home. It was late afternoon when he called and I smiled. He gave me his phone number and asked if we could meet at the park later. This suggested that if we had outside contact three or four more times, he could call me "CC."

In spite of my prior desire to chill at home today, my response was "Ok, I do not plan to run this evening. What time would you like to meet?"

"Well, if we are not exercising, is 7 o'clock cool? I will be done with all working commitments at that time and I can solely concentrate on you."

"That's cool. I will see you then."

"Thank you Crystal, I will see you then."

Ending the phone call I thought only of HOPE.

The time was approaching and I decided to wear nice casual clothing with my primo shoes. Arriving at the park, he was sitting on "our" bench. He stood to greet me and I thought that he was more attractive and enticing than our first encounter.

We sat and conversed. We took a leisurely hand-held walk around the park. Self thought: This evening with him was placid, offering me immense satisfaction with his presence. Suddenly, he delicately pulled me closely toward him and said, "I was hoping that we could go to a movie and dinner. We could consider this a triple date evening and then I can begin to call you CC." (I thought he was going to try kissing me and I would have welcomed it.) I responded, "You think we will be friends after this evening?"

"I can only continue to yearn."

We enjoyed a movie, then dinner at his restaurant. The family business name was Vinson Palace. He explained to me in detail the family members' roles and duties. His responsibilities involved the daily operations and were demanding, and his "work hours" varied depending on the need of the restaurant. The eatery offered a polite atmosphere and the food was delightful. It became very late and he offered a cab for me, but feeling more relaxed with his presence, I stated that he could take me home. Exiting the car and anticipating a "Good night" kiss, he simply said, "Goodnight CC." His suaveness was charming (should I have been alarmed?) but I was not repelled, responding "Good night Phoenix, I will call you tomorrow."

" I most definitely wish you would."

FAST FORWARD TWELEVE MONTHS AND A FEW DAYS

We had consummated our "relationship" several months prior.

I know, I know-same chick who did not want this.

I know, I know-same chick that deprived intimacy to rebuild herself.

I know, I know-same chick who did not want to live, for taking another breath was strenuous.

I KNOW, I KNOW, I AM THAT CHICK!

Realizing he was a better man, this time the texture and sensation of HIS touch made me feel worthy of the Happiness and Love he promised to bring to my world. Our relationship was stupendous and blossoming wondrously.

We began to intermingle with our family and friends. We made a treaty that bi-monthly was family-friend time and twice per month would be "our bonding time." My peeps gave their stamp of approval (which facilitated my immersion and enthusiasm in our relationship.)

It was our time with his family. His parents expressed their acceptance with me and they were always good-natured toward me. We arrived at their home with his brother and sister-in-law (Frankie and Beverly) awaiting our arrival to start the usual mess—talking, card-playing and drinking, as his parents prepared dinner for everyone. Our dinner conversations would vary and the discussion for this evening was employment (at his initiation.) It was revealed that I was unemployed (which until this very moment did not make me feel "less than.") He stated in his polished delivery, "An employed woman is intriguing." Of course, I instantaneously thought—then what the hell does that make me? I was not offended, but somewhat displeased, with the comment.

On the way to his home we drove in silence except for the radio playing. Self-thought: he is very astute and I am sure he knows I am in my feelings. He did not want to humiliate me, but why is he giving me the silent treatment? Finally— I asked,

"What is wrong with you?"

"I'm not aware of anything that is wrong, at least not with me. Do you have a problem of any kind?"

"No, I do not have a problem but there is...." But before I could continue, he abruptly said, "OK, there are no problems, no need for you to make any for us."

With an astounded look, I replied "I had no intentions on making any problems for us."

Sarcastically, he replied "Good."

He arrived at my house and that was the end of the discussion. I exited the car bewildered at what just happened.

Initially when he made the comment—should I have remarked at that moment? Should I learn not to let things fester and straighten them out with the straight away—right away?

Should I have begun the conversation with expressing how his comments made ME catch a vibe that was unpleasant?. Should I have not posed a question so that he could validate my vibe and mood?

Did I permit him the authority to turn the focus on how HE should not be upset with ME?

Should I have insisted that it was not the end of the discussion considering I did not express the intended conversation.

Should I have asked the pertinent question, "If employed women are intriguing, tell me how you feel about ME? Am I no longer appealing or intriguing to you?"

LASTLY, I SHOULD HAVE ASKED, "WHY THE HELL DID YOU BRING ME HOME WHEN I WANT TO BE WITH YOU?

< WALKING AWAY DEFICIENCY AROSE WITHIN <

No one was home when I arrived. My Dad was working and Mom was probably visiting my Grandma or my Sister. While bathing, I called Stephanie and we had girl talk for a couple of hours. I was in the bath until my fingertips were wrinkled.

It was an unusual ambiance on this night. I was oblivious to the imminent anguish that I would before long endure. I fell asleep and was awakened with the sound of the phone ringing. It was Mom informing me that she was at the hospital with my expectant Sister, Patti Louise. She was having complications. I asked how Patti was doing and "Not good at the moment" was her response. Our call was disconnected and as I hung up the phone I noted that it had been several hours that Phoenix had not called. I decided to call him—no answer which is peculiar because he should be home. We always spend overnight at his home when it is family/friends time. I called again. Still no answer. Where could he be and is he yearning for me? I hung up and waited and waited and waited. There was a significant time lag until the phone rang again. (About Damn Time His Ass Called Me.) It was Mom calling to tell me that she would be at the hospital until Patti awakens, and when my dad calls tell him to come immediately to the hospital instead of home. Time travel without speaking to Phoenix was mentally detrimental and disturbing. I decided to have a glass of brandy to ease the discomfort. I become easily intoxicated as I am not a brandy drinker. Soon afterward, I experienced a bottommost sleep.

I awoke in my befuddled condition with the distant sound of the phone ringing. All at once, the phone was ringing and my dad was yelling my name. I wrestled to fully awaken and answer my dad and the phone. Lastly, I entered the living room as my dad had a look of worriment.

He asked, "Have you been home for a while?"

"Yes, I have been sleeping."

"I tried calling three times to tell you that I would be staying late at work—so you can tell your mom. Your mom wanted me at the hospital instead of coming home." Solemnly, he said with his head lowered , " I wish I had known. I was not there for them."

Trying to conceal my intoxication, I softly asked, "Dad are you going to visit Patti?"

"Patti and the baby are no longer with us—they died. Your mom called shortly after I arrived home. Patti left us about two hours ago and I was not there for anyone." He started to weep (I had not seen my Dad weep before now.)

I was immobile, mortified, flabbergasted and completely astounded.

WHAT THE FUCK HAVE I DONE?

I gradually and silently walked away.

WHAT THE FUCK HAVE I DONE?

My Phoenix preoccupation made me have a lapse in judgment. Had I not gotten drunk I would have heard the phone ringing and answered. My dad called to let us know he was going to be staying at work later—I would have told him to go to the hospital. My mom had been calling to let me know Patti was gone with the baby and I was too inebriated.

I started to shout "No, No, No this cannot be." I ran throughout the house shouting the same. Finally, I came to a standstill for a long while and sobbed. I made a cup of tea and sat at the table in stillness until my mom arrived. My head was throbbing and my heart was inflated with anguish—and I wanted to speak. My mom stood glaring at me—which was alarming. My lips parted and she sternly and unsympathetically said, "Please Crystal, do not talk to me right now—please not now." I stood and looked at my dad, my lips parted and he said with an injured voice, "Goodnight baby, just goodnight" and he began to weep.

I TURNED AND WALKED AWAY.

Had you asked me two years prior, I would have told you the pain of heartache I experienced was the superior pain. Until now I thought I had experienced the most horrible pits of LOVE. Patti was not only my sister, she was also my best friend. She was the eldest and did not concur with all of my decisions but she always conveyed her unconditional love for me. Now she was GONE— DEAD. Who would I talk to for guidance? Who would I call in my dark hours? It occurred to me that this was the next chapter of my life which was >>>>>>>>>>>>>

T   H   E

E   N   D

I awoke the next morning, lying in bed reflecting on my life with Patti and how I would never come in contact with that special sisterly love again. Patti had moved away from home when she married. We would talk a couple of times per week and we would see one another a few times per month.   They were expecting their first born. I was unaware of any complications so their sudden demise was shocking.

I was anxious approaching the living quarters. My parents were not home which made me uneasy. I called Mama Cicely (my Grandmother.)

"Hello"

"Hi Mama Cicely, are Mama and Dad there?"

In a very monotone voice she responded, "No Crystal, they are not." Silence and tension followed.

"Ok, I just woke and they are not here and did not awaken me."

"I suppose they are making arrangements, and why the hell would they awaken you?"

Panic arose within me because I realized why everyone was displeased with me. They predicted my minimum liability with being constructive to relay any and all pertinent messages. Minimally to stay alert and not be in a drunken state (although, they did not know of my intoxication which amplified their disappointment as to why I was home and could not answer incoming calls.) How could I allow this to happen, and now that it has, how can I confess? Tearfully, I said the only words I could assemble. "Mama Cicely, I'm sorry." Her next words would penetrate my entire being and send me into a deep depression.

"INDEED, YOU ARE SORRY." SHE HUNG UP!

I felt lost and alone, I knew if Mama Cicely was disappointed, my parents were also. I did not know what to do. I made a cup of tea—always somewhat soothing for me. I wanted to talk with a friend and I wanted not to be home when my parents returned. It was mid morning and still NO CALL FROM PHOENIX! I CALLED-NO ANSWER, I CALLED-NO ANSWER!

Now, I am angry, this Mutha Fucka should have called me. It has been longer than 12 hours and this Mutha Fucka is a no call no show. I wanted and needed him so I ignored the obvious turmoil, commotion and havoc that would soon surface, and I called him again.

Finally, he said, "Hello." I was very displeased with him but I was too weak, dismayed and saddened for a fracas.

"Hi, I have called you several times."

"We have inventory this week and last night was a late night because of it. I missed you."

"Yeah, sure you do. If you missed me, you should have called me before now, so spare me the rah rah bullshit." He was silent and then hung up on me. I stood dumbfounded. I decided to make a cup of tea.

Sipping on tea and shedding tears. The doorbell rang and I slowly walked to open the door--IT WAS HIM! Wiping the tears , I opened the door and walked away. He grabbed my arm and pulled me toward him. He asked if my parents were home and I said "no." Once realizing we were home alone, he began whispering in my ear, giving me instructions as he guided me to my bedroom. I sensed that he recognized my need for him to console me without my verbal clarification. He displayed a peculiar demanding tone. It was firm and safe. It made me apprehensive and calm.   It was ambiguous and transparent. I thought to myself, this is very BIZARRE!

He sat on the bed and instructed me to undress and look into his eyes. I did. He looked intently at me, "Come here." I stood in front of him completely exposed and began to quiver with tears. He began aggressively kissing my entire body also kissing my tears away. When I attempted to speak he covered my mouth and tossed me on the bed. He made hot and passionate love to me. He was in total control of me and did with me as he desired (whatever he desired, whatever sexually deviant fantasy he wanted fulfilled—it was that day.) My yearning was to be secure in our love and strangely after this bizarre episode, I felt that he was sexually indifferent toward and with me. It was a perplexing moment as we held one another. There was an intense awkwardness of this sexual experience. We had delved into uncharted territory and I was too consumed with guilt and grief to question any of his actions. Lastly, I spoke about Patti's demise. There were several minutes of silence when our eyes met. He instructed me to get dressed and I DID!

ONE WOULD RATHER DENY LOSS THAN TO ACCEPT

THE INEVITABILITY OF DEATH

It was late afternoon when we arrived at the restaurant. It was quiet and calm before the dinner customers arrived. As he did inventory I sat at the bar watching television. Deliveries started to arrive, and the phone started to ring with customers making reservations. I needed something to occupy my time and thoughts. I wanted to not feel voidness but value. Phoenix came to me and asked if I wanted to help until the host arrived. The restaurant doors opened at 5pm, and it was around 2:00pm. I started to answer the phone for reservations. I took the initiative to perform other tasks such as the table place settings, filling the salt/pepper shakers, folding the napkins and table cloths and organizing the linen closet. Phoenix allowed me to delegate the cleaning assignment. The two-person crew under my direction had Vinson Place done quicker than the usual allotted time. Phoenix observed me working and commented that he was very pleased.

Diana and Arsenio, the hostess and host, arrived. They were uniformly dressed with the summer colors of the restaurant. We began talking and I told them about my answering the phones for reservations. They examined the bookings and were pleased—they asked Phoenix if I could continue taking the calls. I wanted to continue because it engrossed my thoughts. He allowed me to continue. After some time, Phoenix took me into the office and asked if I wanted to return home. I became overwhelmed with emotion and asked if I could have a few moments alone in the office. He told me to take all the time I needed and closed the door behind him. I collected myself and called home. I knew everyone there was disappointed with me and I was distressed not knowing what type of reception I would receive. Anxiously, I called. After ringing several times, my Mom answered.

"Hello"

"Hi Mama." A brief uneasy silence followed.

"How are you and Dad doing?" She gave the phone to my Dad.

My voice quivering, I asked, Dad are you and Mama upset with me?"

"Where are you?" he asked.

"I am with Phoenix and I want to come home."

My dad was always the empathetic and loving being.

"Come home if you want to come home baby."

Vinson Place was active and Phoenix was with the patrons. I called a cab and told Phoenix that I was leaving and would call him later. I arrived home and could hear my parents quarreling (about me.) When I opened the door, the quarreling ceased. I stood in the doorway until my Dad asked, "Baby, would you like some tea with me?"

"Yes, I would." I approached my mom, gave her a hug, and whispered, "Please do not be angry with me, I'm sorry."

She gave a disconcerting look as she began to whimper and leave the house to visit Mama Cecily. My Dad and I sat at the table sipping on tea in silence. At last, I asked, "Dad are you angry with me?"

"No."

"Is Mama?"

"I think she is more disappointed than angry."

"Are the funeral arrangements done?"

"Your Mama and Grandma are taking care of that. It will be in a couple of days. You look tired. Go to bed and rest." I apperceived that my Dad was not angry and also disappointed, although he would not say such words in this time to me. I excused myself and went to my room.

As I lay in bed, music softly playing, the phone rang. It was Phoenix—I was elated with fatigue. He asked how were things going, and I gave him an update. "Will you go to the funeral with me?" I asked.

"CC, I do not go to funerals, but I will make an exception. I must work late for the rest of the week to make allowance for that day. As a matter of fact, I will work late tonight because we are getting very busy."

"Okay, call me tonight when you're done. I want and need to be with you."

"It will be late and you will be asleep."

"Still I would like for you to call."

"Alright, I will call you later."

We hung up and an unnerving vibe came to me. We had been dating for a few of years and I had come to a space within our relationship that gave me joy. When we met I was in an unwholesome and injured place in my life. I scrutinized my being and was determined not to make the same mistakes. I identified my flaws and exhausted months of self-improving labor so that I could be a better woman for a man. I would not allow my doubtfulness and mistrust of love producing heartache derail my happiness with this man. Throughout our time, I no longer resisted our happiness and loving him.

Yes, tonight I need him to need me as I need him, love me as I love him. I want him to know that I am strong because he strengthens me, I am happy because he is my happiness. Tonight, verbalization of love will not be required. I will unleash all of my physical, emotional and mental energy for his consumption and desire. He is deserving of my complete and unadulterated self. Furthermore, it is because of him loving me that my life will be forever changed.

My mom returned home and she was awkwardly cordial with me. I was hopeful that she would curse, lash out – even shun me. Then I could apologize for my unspeakable priority. I felt the uncouthness but was too lost, confused, unaccounted for and unrecognized to verbalize my feelings. I had experienced pain and I believed those would be my darkest days. These were darker and the loneliest days—coupled with absolute melancholy. I could only hope that my family would give me the opportunity to convey my REMORSE.

She sat at the table and began writing notes for the obituary. I acquired courage to ask, "What day is the service?" She glimpsed at me and said, "Three days." That would be Friday. We then looked at one another and my lips parted and I said, "Mama, I'm sorry for everything I did. I loved Patti and the baby, and I love my family." Lowering her head she responded, "Crystal, I know you loved and they loved you as I always will." Silence lingered and I wanted to be with her so I continued to sit at the table sipping on tea. After an hour, she stood and softly said, "I will see you in the morning. Good night."

I began to think of my journey with Phoenix and how at this moment our relationship seemed somewhat indifferent. He had not called and it was approximately 2:00 AM. How late would it be before I received a call? It appeared that he was not as attentive in these past months. I recognized it and did not want to generate unrest in our relationship. There were times he would make me be of the opinion that I had done something wrong—when I had not. At times, his reaction and commentary to situations were abrasive. Often times I would ignore it, or give an offhand response. He was aware of my history with love and loss. He was aware of my fragility when we met and how vital it was for me to have it right with him. We conversed about all subjects and cultivated our friendship for months. He assured me that he was not a philanderer and that he wanted the same relationship quality as I. He made me content with his actions, especially loving me. He has been good to and for me. I entrusted him with my deepest trepidation and relinquished myself to him. Now I yearn to make him forever happy and to love him for a lifetime.

It was dawn and my eyes opened to his gentle touch and kiss. I remarked, "How nice it is for you to make time for me, and how long have you been here?" I went to rise from my position and he encased me with his body and we lay there in stillness. He began to hold me firmly and I began to sob. He softly spoke, "What do you want or need from me?" I wanted to discuss his infrequent calling and response time these days, but was overcome with concern about his responsive action. I remained silent.

"I talked to your peeps and they told me what they needed." My parents were fond of Phoenix, thinking that he was a commendable man. I asked, "What do they need from you?"

"They would like me to take care of you."

"Well, to do that, you may have to call and make yourself available which appears to be a difficulty these days."

"CC, you should know that I am available for you."

"Phoenix, you have been distant, neglectful and at times unapproachable before Patti died—months before.

I left you early yesterday evening and have not heard or seen you...." He abruptly covered my mouth with his hand. "Knowing that you and your peeps need to talk and be with one another at this time, I did not want to monopolize your time." Furthermore, it was an extremely busy day at the restaurant and lastly, I called you at closing and your mom told me that you were sleeping. I asked if I could come over to talk with them and they allowed me and here I am. I will ask you again. What do you need and want from me?" Needless to say, I was content with his response. Although it was an irregular vibe, he was here with me and that was sufficient.

"Would you stay with me?"

"Is that what you need me to do?"

"Yes."

"I have only one stipulation."

"What is it?"

"I must plan our day." I agreed to the stipulation.

He instructed me to get dressed for the day while he talked with my parents. He returned and told me that my peeps had left to take care of arrangements. I was half dressed and his demeanor slightly changed. He approached me and started to kiss my cheek, lips, neck, breast. I started to lie on the bed and he authoritatively instructed me to remain standing. I began to express my remorse regarding Patti's and the baby's demise. I began to express to him how I felt deserted and remorseful due to my distraction because of him. The more I expressed, the more vehement he would apply his tongue to my body. Continuing to kiss me with his tongue as an apparatus, he forcibly but lovingly ripped my skirt to shreds as he whispered "where do you need my tongue and if you need it plead for it." At this moment I was astounded and weakened with intense sexual arousal. I was timid with anticipation of this sexual encounter. Timidly and low I said, "I need you and I love you."

With agitation and annoyance he stepped away and began to leave the bedroom.

Frantically, I said, "I need your tongue."

He turned to face me and said, "What did you say?"

"I need your tongue."

"I cannot hear your words."

Louder, I repeated "I need your tongue. I need your tongue."

Contemptuously he demanded that I plead for it.

"Please, Phoenix I need your tongue."

"Louder." He demanded.

"Please give it to me."

"Louder and plead for it." He came closer and our eyes met, he wiped my tears and repeated his words.

Submissively, I screeched and begged him to give me his tongue.

He instructed me to turn with my back toward him and face the mirror on my headboard.

He ferociously plunged his well-endowed penis into me. I screamed with panic and pain. He exhaustively made love to me for what seemed like 2 hours. Unconditionally, I gave myself and satisfied all of his deviant sexual appetite. Afterward, he said, "Now I need your tongue." Without hesitation or question, I satisfied him with my tongue.

Later, I lie in ambivalence to what transpired. I wanted and needed to feel as if this session was special and distinguished from all others. I lie there silently trembling with discouragement and glee. As we showered, I cried. Then, we made love again and again until I was depleted of all energy. He asked after showering, "Are you ready to begin our journey."

"Yes."

"Take my hand and we shall start."

I grabbed onto him, and he to me. We kissed as we tasted my salty tears, and in this moment we were one.

I packed for overnight. I left a note for my parents that I would call soon to check in. As we walked hand-in-hand to the front door, I stopped and stood, gazing at my surroundings, feeling as if this would be the ultimate feeling of belonging. As we drove away from my home, there was a disconnect in my being but I was too fragile to question.

We arrived at a mall. Exiting the car, I was numb and robotic. This man was a necessity to and for me at this moment. He was a fundamental extension of my existence. I noticed him awkwardly looking at me. I contemplated broaching the subject of our relationship and its growing-pain moments, which I believed left loving scars that strengthened our bond. It was our time to experience extreme joy. I would not deny this moment of me loving him and he here for me.

We entered the mall, and with his arm around me, he led us to a bench. I sat as he stood, He then asked with a staid tone:

"What attire would you prefer for your initial employment?"

"What are you talking about?"

"I was busy yesterday creating a position for you with Vinson Place."

With astonishment I asked, "Why?"

"The hostess center is a good initial opportunity for you. You need this, and now is the time."

We sat and discussed the particulars of my job responsibilities. Baffled at the longest first interview of my life, I accepted the position as hostess.

*****ALL RESERVATIONS I HAD ABOUT HIM DISSOLVED IN THIS MOMENT***** HE IS MY LIFE PARTNER AND WITH HIM I WILL NEVER BE ALONE****

After shopping we arrived at his place. We continued discussing employment details. I was to start next week on a part-time basis with a weekly wage. There could be no monetary reward for this sense of security, gift of love and the Phoenix experience—I would have hosted free of charge.

We were enjoying this happy occasion with one another. Suddenly, his phone rang and he took the call to another part of the house. His voice was barely audible and the call seemingly created uneasiness within. I cannot describe the why or how—only that it did. I carried the fault for this sentiment—it was me, so I needed to delete.

As if he knew I was going to comment on the call, he entered the room and began to romance me--AGAIN! His aptitude in the sexual category always received my undivided attention and rendered me thoughtfully unconscious. To show my gratitude and confess my love was my desire, and all his desires were my quest. This love-making session was also very intense. I would describe it as a love-making mangled fest.   We were awakened by the doorbell a few hours later. He got dressed and I lay in awe before calling home—there was no answer. I was dressing when Phoenix called to me, "CC, you have visitors, Frankie and Beverly." His brother and wife came to visit. I joined them and his brother gave me a hug. "Congratulations and welcome to this thing called work." He had the application and other paperwork for me to complete before my start date.

Frankie and Phoenix were co-managers, but Phoenix was the more dedicated brother to the business. Frankie would contribute but mostly reaped the benefits of Phoenix's hard work and commitment to the family business. There was a silent suspicion among them that Phoenix would inherit the business. We chattered and laughed until Frankie offered to operate the restaurant tonight, allowing Phoenix and me the opportunity to celebrate the entire evening. Beverly poured champagne and we toasted to my sister, her baby, and my future. There was an uncomfortable silence when Frankie proposed to take the evening shift. It was as if Phoenix was taken aback by the suggestion, and hesitation resulted. Beverly broke the silence with her ability to diffuse a situation and said, "It appears the brothers should bond at work. The sister-in-laws can bond and celebrate." In my opinion, Frankie and Beverly were a couple that engaged in contentious banter. They seemed loving and were individuals who seemed comfortable with their individuality with or without one another. Beverly was a sharp shooter. She was always in her comfort zone—wrong, right, or indifferent, and seldom apologetic. With a tinge of insecurity I said, "That's cool Beverly, let's do it." We kissed the guys and were out the door.

This was our first time spending one-on-one time together. We would chatter at family gatherings, but not an extended period of time. As we were driving she would make references to Phoenix and Frankie, but more so Phoenix.   No   comments   were   derogatory··merely generalizations.

I suspected that she was alerting me all was not as it appeared. Our day went forth conversing on a variety of topics—family,   friends,   love,   life,   death,   and   our respective relationships with the brothers. She ended on the note, "Both are a trip, but Phoenix got some extra shit with him." Beverly and I enjoyed the day together. It was late evening when she took me home. It was a draining day, and fast to sleep I went.

The next couple of days passed swiftly. While at the funeral reminiscing over Patti's love it was inconceivable that I would no longer have her grace to embrace. The service was exhausting and challenging—I decided that I would not attend any future funerals. The repass was hosted at Mama Cecile's home and unbeknownst to me Vinson's Place catered. Phoenix's mom/dad, Beverly and Frankie attended. His mother and father made a brief appearance to ensure the catering and two servers had arrived promptly. Beverly had agreed to help serve and clean up. I was not informed that they were doing this, and I was overwhelmed with gratitude and indebtedness. Phoenix, Frankie and his parents left after things were properly set up and food was served. Of course, his reason was he had to get back to the restaurant because of short staffing—which I understood.   I was filled with such appreciation that, when he hugged me, I began to weep and utter the words "thank you and I love you very much." Beverly remained with me until the end. We cleaned and packaged the dishware to be returned.   Once done, Beverly looked a t the time and said, "It is 2 AM now, what would you like to do?"

"I wish Phoenix did not have to work late tonight. I would like to see him."

"He was not forced to work late. I suppose he enjoys working late."

"Actually, he had to get back because of short staffing. He went above and beyond for me today." She was silent for seconds and then said, "Well, it was his parents that went above and beyond consenting to the catering. Without their consent those boys cannot do anything. Although, most people assume it is Phoenix's place—it is not. He did not go above and beyond, only did what should have been expected of him." It was as though she was trying to have me acknowledge and accept that I was worthy of good, better and the best. At times she would become agitated when speaking of the guys--especially Phoenix. This was one of those times.

I responded, "Nonetheless, Beverly I am grateful."

"Cool, be grateful, but no need to think he went above and beyond." We looked at each other and I smiled. "Thanks Bev for being with me today." In classic Beverly fashion she responded, "Now I deserve the damn above and beyond trophy." Laughter erupted from both of us as we hugged. I decided to go to Vinson Place to see Phoenix. I desired his presence and more so his touch. Trying to understand her subtle comments I asked as we were riding, "Beverly do you totally love Frankie?" With a fleeting look at me, she responded, "Indeed, I do but not to my detriment." There was silence for the remainder of the ride.

As we arrived at the parking lot, I noticed Phoenix walking someone to their car—which was not unusual considering the late hour. I do not think Beverly noticed due to her lack of comment. Frankie came to us as we entered and led us to a table. It was approximately 20 minutes when Beverly asked, "Where is Phoenix?" Frankie said, "He is around here, probably in the kitchen or doing paperwork."

"Does he know CC is here?"

"Probably not, sweetheart."

Soon after their exchange Phoenix joined us at the table. He asked why I was out so late after a long day?

"I needed to be with you tonight."

"Really, you need and not want me? Actions speak volumes. Maybe you will show me later." I concentrated on his face and eyes. Whereas we had humorous banter in our relationship, I did not think this was a time for it. I was perplexed at this of conversational mood, but I was too emotionally fragile for the battle. Undeniably, I wondered could this be due to his 30-minute escort of a patron to **HER** car. I opted to respectfully yield and change the course of the conversation.

"Should I complete the paperwork for my employment tonight, or are you too busy?"

"Actually, you can go into my office."

I excused myself from the table and we went into his office. As I was completing the application, he received a business call on one of the two office phones. I thought patrons were calling with compliments or complaints of service and he implied as much. Without warning an intoxicated woman appeared in the doorway, and with an antagonistic posture said, "I would like to speak with the Manager—and that would be you about damages to my car while on your premises." He hung up from the call, jotting down a phone number and telling the patron that he would call them back soon. Somewhat perplexed, he walked toward the woman and said, "Certainly, let's go look at the damage." She stood there for a few seconds angrily focused on him, and he softly spoke, "after you."

I thought to self: this is the woman I saw him escorting to her car. Maybe that's why he remained outdoors for a time. Perhaps she damaged the car while leaving. His customer service was first-rate. I completed the application and sat thinking about Patti—how she would be proud of my first employment opportunity. There was a knock at the door. Beverly entered and asked if I was done and if I wanted her to take me home. I told her that I would be staying with Phoenix. She gave me a hug and said, "we will talk tomorrow." "Thanks for all you did Beverly. Goodnight." I thought of Beverly as a cool, cordial woman and today, she became my friend. Today cemented our mutual respect for one another, our sisterhood connection intensified and I was delighted that we had befriended each other.

I was asleep in the oversized chair when he returned to the office. I awoke to him affectionately kissing and massaging me. Not permitting me to move, we kissed the longest we had ever. Once done, I stood and he firmly held me and wordlessly commanded my complete submission. My entire body was moist and craved his love. He placed my hand on his genitals. "Do you want him inside of you?"

"Absolutely, I do." He lifted my dress and discovered my moistness. His fingers nestled inside me as he observed me panting and pleading for more. Unexpectedly he halted the finger pleasuring and said, "Go to my house and get ready for more pleasure." The only words I could muster were "OK" and off I went in the restaurant cabbie. Temporarily evading my grief for a healthier mood, I wanted this night to be special. I had more love to release and display—I wanted to show him more that my love is forever his. I began to converse with

Goldie—the cabbie. We discussed me working with Phoenix and how happy I was to be employed. He let me know that he had a contract with the business and he would pick me up and take me home for work when needed. I thanked him as I got out of the cab.

I took a long bath and grappled with my thoughts. I would immensely miss my sister Patti—our bond, her wisdom, support, guidance and mostly her love of me. She was not only my SIBLING, she was my FRIEND. I thought about calling my parents, then thought it was very late and decided to emerge myself into a love gratification session with Phoenix that would simply unify and solidify our love.

I awoke at sunrise to his stroke. As I turned to face him, I suppressed any trepidation regarding the hour and we began our sexual expedition that lasted until mid-morning. It was a bizarre and fantastic session—as I executed his every desire and request. As I rose to make breakfast, he said "I want some more." I gave him a repeat satisfying performance. Afterward, I rose with glee and thorough exhaustion as he peacefully slept. He awoke a few hours later and went to take a shower. I entered the shower and began washing his back and he washed my body. As the warm water poured over us, I said to him, "I can only hope that you know how much I love you, how much I want and need you in my life forever." I repeated several times, "I love you" because it was imperative that he knew. He compassionately responded, "I know you do Baby and I love you."

XOXOXO···MISSION ACCOMPLISHED···XOXOXO

We sat with robes, drinking tea and listening to music. It was a beautiful summer afternoon. We conversed for hours—we pledged our love and commitment for one another. We confided to one another about ourselves and the highs and lows with family. I told him about the evening Patti left me and how I was preoccupied with thoughts and disappointment that I had not spoken with him. I told him that I got boozed up and fell into an unconscious sleep state and did not hear the phone calls regarding the grave situation, and that now I feel alone as an outsider. He assured me that I was not alone because we have each other.

With our morning activities, exhaustion overcame me and I could no longer resist sleep. I awoke, surprisingly, to find Phoenix gone. It was time for me to go home and check on the family. As I was dressing, the phone rang and it was him. He explained that he received an alarm notice at the business. Once there he needed to stay, as it was opening hours. He also had to do payroll with his dad and Frankie. I told him how I was going to spend the rest of my day and that I would be here when he got off work.

SEVEN MONTHS 25 DAYS—SINCE PATTI'S DEPARTURE

It was now winter, and as the weather became colder, my thoughts grew disconnected. I was silently muddling through my guilt. I began to sink in daily regrets about Patti and my niece or nephew. It was an uncanny atmosphere at home—it was not overt hostility, but an obvious remoteness had occurred with my parents. Although they demonstrated love it was a difficult time for all.

It was this season that Phoenix and I embarked on a live-in relationship. I believed the timing and flow with us was good quality. During my grieving he was the pillar and became the principal determination for my effort and existence. Usually, my days were occupied with the restaurant—I was working full-time hours and I enjoyed it. At times we would spend the entire day working together.

FIVE YEARS of loving and living together passed. At long last, I began to embrace laughter and happiness without guilt. I made every effort to be the exceptional woman. Maxwell's song—WHENEVER, WHEREVER, WHATEVER was the way I lived with and for Phoenix. His every desire was my objective to satisfy. Undeniably I had reached my destination of longevity and life with him···I WAS CONTENT AND ALL WAS WELL!

Business was thriving with Vinson Place. Phoenix's parents would often express their approval and satisfaction with my hostess position. His mom, Phyllis, would meet with me monthly to discuss business. Repeatedly, my curiosity arose when we would spend two or three hours together, conferring about life, love, relationships, shopping etc. At the conclusion of all conversations, she would say, "You are a strong and good woman. Always keep your head to the sky and believe in your goodness and strength." During one of our many meetings, I suggested that we should give back and demonstrate appreciation for the customers. She agreed and stated, "I have noticed that you have good interpersonal connections with the customers. Some customers have complimented on your service. If you want the project it is yours." Immediately, following our meeting I started planning a customer appreciation week. It was a consuming and tiresome eight-week process. I worked tirelessly to ensure that it would be a success.

I was familiar with the regular customers. We would have pleasantries as they were seated. The woman who had car damage a long while ago was also a regular patron. Rarely would I seat her. Usually, she would order a drink at the bar with Phoenix as the server. Phoenix was an attractive, genial and smooth operator with swag. It was his business to cater and provide a delightful experience to all customers. Often, he would treat the flirtatious women with respect and distance. Some customers were aware of our relationship. We agreed to no PDA and always maintained professionalism. At discreet times, we would make eye contact, and he would wink. There would be rare moments in the office of a kiss or gentle touch.

There was a transition of sorts with us, I thought not in an awful way but things were shifting with our relationship. We no longer exercised together—due to our work schedules. We dedicated ourselves to work until it started to seem as if we were professional without a personal relationship. Each time I attempted to discuss my concerns, he would spin my words and accuse me of accusing him without justification. He would say, "You should express more gratitude and less suspicion."

Arguments about his behavior set in motion his anger and leaving home until the early morning hours. I was stricken with depression whenever he was not pleased with me. Of course, upon his return regardless of the hour, I would apologize and then show my gratitude— usually with a sexual act to satisfy him.

On this day I arrived at work and Phoenix was serving at the bar. I observed a regular patron take a seat at the bar. As Phoenix served her I noticed she was agitated. They were making small talk and she became less agitated. I felt that something was not kosher at the moment. I asked Phoenix if we could discuss a discrepancy with reservations (as that was my code for "we need to discuss your bullshit.") Knowing this, he declined my request and suggested that he was certain I could handle things. After a few seconds elapsed with me glaring at him and with a stern tone I responded, "certainly, I shall handle it, but we need to speak at your earliest convenience." I was angry but maintained restraint. Dinner reservations kept me on the go for several hours. There was a peculiarity in the atmosphere and I was weakened with displeasure. At the end of my shift I asked the cabbie to take me home. The ride was silent until he asked, "Are you ok tonight?"

"I'm alright, just a little tired. Why do you ask?"

"You just seem a little down."

"Well, I have been keeping long hours getting everything ready for customer appreciation week."

"Do you have everything ready?"

"Yes, for the most part. I am going to make the announcement in a few days."

"It should be nice. I have heard a few customers speaking of it, and they seem excited."

"That's good, I have a few things planned. I will need Phoenix to give me approval on my agenda before I can make the announcement."

**********Suddenly, the mood and our conversation shifted.**********

Speaking with a tad of tension, he said, "I would think that he would give his approval. No one had done this in the couple of years that I have been a cab driver for them. Customers' feedback is all positive. It would be ridiculous and juvenile not to approve it." He murmured something inaudible. I sensed that he was tense.

Goldie and I would always have pleasant conversations. He would transport me to and from work a few times per week. Often, on the ride home he would tell me different restaurant rider tales—some funny and some not so. He was aware that Phoenix and I had a long-term relationship--he was the cabbie on our initial date. Recognizing that he was somewhat agitated with Phoenix I shifted the conversation to exercising and physical fitness.

I particularly did not want to go home, but knew if I continued working, things would turn disastrous. Impulsively I wanted to run—I needed perspiration out of desperation. Somehow, I yearned for the way things were and the way we were. I wanted to run and keep running until all doubt and anguish would somehow disappear. I asked Goldie if he would drop me off at the park so that I could exercise. He looked confused and he stuttered the words, "Sure, but it is late for a midnight run." For the first time I looked him directly in his eyes and it was in this moment that I realized he had a genuine concern for me with a genuine loving connection. Stunned I said, "I will be fine. It has been weeks and I need to run." I quickly exited the car. As I crossed the threshold of our home, emptiness, disquiet, but mostly trepidation overcame me. With urgency, I dressed for exercising and exited the home.

The ride to the park was unusually silent as I sat in the back. Only words spoken as we arrived to the park was him asking, "What time do you want me to come back for you?"

"In about two hours."

With kindness and discernment, he responded, "Okay, two hours I will return."

I stretched for a few minutes, then I ran and ran and ran! My brain wave was in overload. Reflection and deliberation overwhelmed me—so I ran.

I had become distant from my family because of self-induced guilt that I carry— so I ran.

I had become grief-stricken thinking of my best sister friend Patti— so I ran.

I had become a shell of a person that allowed my man to consume me for only his personal gain—so I ran.

I thought about my niece or nephew and how they would have been a delight and contribution to the world had they survived—so I ran.

I thought of all the wasteland that my life had become—so I ran.

I thought of Phoenix and how my life was transformed and always in a problematic way—so I ran.

I thought about damaged goods, a wounded heart, injured and neglected in the name of love—so I ran.

I ran with every degree of energy within. I hoped for reconstruction, love and closure with all being in my life. I began to weep as I sprinted my last two laps.

As my run came to an end, Goldie was not here for my return ride. I decided to walk to my parents' and call a cab to go home.   While walking the path and preparing myself, I experienced zooming mental moments. I made the unwavering decision to enter the home with love and remorse. I had not seen my parents for about a month— I would call weekly but had stayed distant in visiting. I wanted unspoken forgiveness and I could not forgive myself for my selfish love.

As I was approaching the intersection, I heard a repeat horn blowing and someone calling out "CC, CC." I crossed the intersection and looked in the direction--It was MY EX LOVE. I had not seen him in many years, nor was I prepared.   I utterly froze for seconds! My only thought was: What the fuck is happening? My world seemed to be crumbling because inwardly I knew that my life with Phoenix was in jeopardy.   Despite the fact, I function better in denial. If there would ever be a good time to see him, now is not the time. I was grateful for perspiration as I ran because he parked the car a distance ahead and was walking toward me. I could not muster any movement, still frozen. "Help Me!" I roared within. I gained some equanimity and as if not to hear my name called, I turned in the opposite direction and started to run. I ran with speed and until I could not sense him. I wanted the security of Phoenix and I ran to our home. It was 2:30am when I arrived on the doorstep. I walked into the yard and sat to regain myself. This was very unusual for me. I had not been out so late without him or his knowing my whereabouts. Nervously, I slowly unlocked the door to enter our home. It was as I left it –Phoenix was not home. I was concerned but also relieved—I ran a bath. The home was empty and dark except for the candles surrounding the tub. Meditating while submerged in water, there was a sensation of commotion with all that had transpired. Physically and mentally fatigued, I awoke at 7:30am and still no Phoenix.

Stillness absent tranquility was in this home. I resolved to be steadfast in love and with tenacity. I began making breakfast and dinner, yielding to normalcy. I resolved not to be angry, aloof or remote, although I was all of these emotions given the situation—a no-call-no-show that blossomed into "love should have brought your ass home last night." This was absolutely unacceptable and vile. His actions were audacious and not appropriate—and it was mind-boggling. I had to make countless resolutions regarding the previous 24 hours, which were marked by utter disrespect, negligence and total disregard. I resolved not to question why Goldie was not at the park for my return ride home. Why did my encounter my "ex" stimulate sheer and aggressive defenselessness? I resolved not to criticize or become accusatory of the culpability for Phoenix's inappropriateness. I resolved to start over only in the "name of love."

The house was cleaned and dinner was prepared—smothered chicken, rice, broccoli with cheese and biscuits. Scented candles, music and a comforting summertime breeze loomed within the home.

Gradually, the delightful atmosphere diminished as I heard him entering the home. Self-thought: remain calm and resolved. I was sitting on the sofa, listening to music and eating lunch as it was after 12 noon. He closed the door behind him, and with a smug swagger, glanced at me and walked into the kitchen. I patiently consumed my lunch and hesitantly walked into the kitchen. He was sitting at the table drinking a glass of lemonade. The silence was so exceptionally frightening that I cautiously remained silent but amicable. Standing at the sink, I could sense his eyes on me. It was a ghastly vibe as he viewed my back side. I prolonged washing a few dishes with a song—Lenny Williams—"I love you, I need you, I want you." With much apprehension it had come time for our eyes to intersect. I thought I must make a smooth transition, one that permits him no accountability and that will demonstrate my blameless love and commitment to our lives together. This reaction was and had become familiar to me.

Steadily, turning toward him, I asked, "Baby, would you like to have lunch or a taste of dinner?" I swiftly walked toward him with arms open to give him a loving embrace. I grasped him and made the proclamation, "I love you. I need you. I want you, oh, oh, oh, I cannot live without you." My clutch was tense with genuine apologetic love and forgiveness.

Astonishingly, he was unyielding still. I had never experienced such callousness. I released my hold and stepped backward. Our eyes connected and his unspoken detachment was evident. I shuddered with tears as I walked away. Several hours passed as I was in the bedroom and he was not. Ultimately, I rose and he was not in the house. I sat on the sofa until I heard music coming from the outside rear of the house. I followed the sound and he was doing yard work to music. I thought, how odd. He had never done yard work. Usually, we would hire help to do that. As I stood in my shadow observing my surroundings and his demeanor, it occurred to me that Phoenix did not live here any longer. Still not having the fortitude to confront, I walked away within my shadow. I stood by the kitchen window watching him intently—it was as if he was in a remote zone of his own. I began to question my ineffective womanhood.

Assessing the volatility of the moment I made the only effective decision and started to dress for work. I was dressing in the bedroom when he appeared and just stood there, seemingly without sentiment, looking at me. I was too anxious to look at him and too fearful to ignore the obvious. Making a feeble attempt to defuse the awkwardness, I hugged him and said ever so delicately, "I wanted to go to work early and begin making return calls for reservations." I walked past him and did not have any direction, so I escaped to the basement. The basement was silent and refreshing. I stood appreciating the beauty. It was secluded, blameless and with superior silence. I needed the aching to cease in this silence. Yes, undeniably, I am willing to forgive and try to forget in this silence. Of course, we never forget, but we will not utter a word about the discomfort. Let's move forward from this day and in the "name of love" I will maintain and sustain our lives together. He only needs to trust me and believe I will make it happen—just do not prolong this agony. I started to walk toward a section with an always closed door because of the cold draft. As I took my first step in that direction, all of a sudden, he was yelling my name.

IT WAS AS IF HE WAS IN PANIC MODE THINKING I HAD LEFT HIM!

I quickly started organizing a load of clothes to wash, I did not look at him when I said, "I am going to wash this last load before I go to work." My intuition arose and alerted me that his equilibrium was altered and I would soon learn that he would become unrecognizable.

"How are you getting to work?"

"I was going to call a cab or Goldie."

"Do you have money for a cab?"

"Yes, I do. Thanks, Honey for asking."

"Would you pay the bills on your way?"

Trying to obtain some semblance of "the way we were" I responded jokingly, "Well, I do not have that much money." I began to laugh.

"I'm sure you do not as usual."

Silence permeated the room as we stared at one another. Tearfully, I walked past him and said, "Honey, I was joking but I now know we no longer have laughter or humor." As he followed me out of the basement he responded brutishly, "I guess we do not. The money for the bills is on the kitchen table."

He was displaying such revulsion toward me and us— this was unforeseen and upsetting. My sixth sense knew we were at the end of our love, but I did not want to give up or let go. I gathered my things and left. I walked to the store to pay bills before work. There was a long wait for bill paying. When it was my turn I heard someone calling my name—it was Beverly. She approached me and said that she called, and Phoenix told her my whereabouts. She requested that I take a ride with her before work. The ride to her home was silent. I was relieved to be with her.

"CC, you do not look well. Are you ok?" I did not answer because I was full of pain and would explode. We walked into the house and I sat on the sofa. She prepared us a snack and wine platter. She sat beside me and said, "When you are ready to talk about it I am here." I took a sip of wine and said, "thank you," and I began to weep. She went away and returned with a pillow and knitted quilt. She told me to lie on the sofa, I did, and it felt nice with the pillow under my head and the quilt offered warmth. She sat on the floor beside me and said, "My grandma made that quilt for me and it always makes me feel better when I wrap it around me."

"Yes it is nice and soothing."

"Take all the time you need. When you're ready, I'm ready." We laughed as tears fell. She told me, "let it out, let it go. Take your time and cry. I am going to my bedroom and watch television. No need to rush." As she walked away, I wanted to express my gratitude for her concern and kindness. Instead I silently cried myself to sleep. I awoke feeling the consolation of her grandma's made quilt. I heard Beverly's conversation on the phone telling someone that "She probably will not be coming to work this evening because she is not feeling well. Besides, the event is a few weeks away and the majority of the preparation and calls have been made. We have time to make other calls, today or tomorrow. If we come at all it will be later this evening. I will ask her."

I rose with the quilt wrapped around me. As I stood looking out the window, I saw her drive away. I sat on the porch and the warm breeze with sunshine felt good. The porch was set nicely with two rocking chairs, an oversized chair and two portable tray tables. I closed my eyes and thought this is nice to be with Beverly. We seemed to have a sisterly connection and I need a sister. I miss you Patti!

She returned with pizza and cheesecake. She prepared us an attractive tray and said, "Girl, we are about to have ladies night with outside dinner." We ate, drank and listened to music until late in the evening. We remained on the porch and were comfortable enjoying each other. She handed me a small gold box, I began to shiver and did not open it and she did not insist. Lenny Williams' song was playing—"I love you, I want you, etc." I looked at her and said, "The words in this song describe how I feel about Phoenix. I am in pain and do not understand what I did to bring about such pain. I have done and would do any and all things to make him happy—how can he display such disregard for me?" She remained silent and listened. I continued to tell her about the events of the day and prior. She remained silent and listened. I continued to tell her about the beginning of the deterioration of our relationship. She remained silent and listened. I continued to tell her that I did not recognize the man in my life today—how his eyes were rigid and his face indifferent. She remained silent and listened. I continued to tell her about my years of love apprehension, how I completely entrusted him to receive my absolute love and extend reciprocity, because that was his promise for us and mostly for my life. My pain was overpowering and I could not continue to speak as my tears were overflowing. After prolonged silence, she hugged me and whispered, "Do not fault yourself, because it is not you." My last thought was déjà vu, and I collapsed.

I awoke to Beverly's foul mouth and touch. While holding my hand she was cussin' me out. "Girl, what the fuck happened, CC?" If you everrrrrrrrrrrr do that shit again we are going to have a total mutha fuckin' misunderstanding. Now do you understand me?" Then she smiled and asked, "How are you feeling and do you need anything?"

I gazed at my surroundings and realized I was in a hospital room. With soft spoken words I said, "Girl, you ain't never lied. What the fuck did happen? Love knocked me the fuck out I guess." We cried with laughter. The nurse entered and explained to me that I experienced a grief-stricken stress black-out episode. When your heart, mind, body, and soul are consumed with the burdens of stress and grief, sometimes it will short circuit the mind and will cause the body to shut down.... I interrupted with the words "and knock you the fuck out." Beverly and I cried with laughter as the nurse responded, "Basically."

Beverly asked if I wanted to come to her house or go home. As we arrived in front of my home I wondered if Phoenix was upset because I had not been home or to work and it was now 4:30am the next morning. I was too unnerved to ask Beverly if she had notified him. As I was exiting her car I said, "Thanks, Beverly, thanks for everything." In her being Beverly self, she responded, "Sister girl, no thanks needed, just be well. Now get the hell out of my car and get some rest and regardless of what happens take care of yourself and never love to a detriment. Do you need me to do anything at all?" We hugged and I exited.

I quietly closed the door and stood in the living room. With my eyes wide shut I walked toward the bedroom and stood in the doorway. Uncanny silence, loneliness and desertion engulfed the home and when my eyes became wide open there was NO PHOENIX!

I thought, of course, that he was working late. This gave me the opportunity for resting and contemplating our predicament. I relaxed in a hot bath as I served myself tea with bagels. As I lay on the sofa listening to love songs, I wrote him a letter professing my love. Yes, I have so much to say and I will falter with spoken word. Indeed, if he reads without disturbance he will be cognizant of the fact that we belong together, how much I adore him—every ounce and inch of his person I simply adore with love. Indeed, this love letter is our resolution. This revelation gave me a momentary joyful feeling.

With closed eyes I began to write—I cannot remember my life before you and I cannot imagine my life without you! I believe you losing me would be a mistake and I know me losing you would be disastrous for my life. On bended knee I ask for your love and I will pledge you my life! The End

I placed the sealed letter visibly and I went into the basement. I awoke several hours later around 12 noon. I did not hear any movement upstairs. Oddly, I thought this was good, thinking after a long work evening, he had read my letter and that it had unruffled our situation, allowing him the opportunity to realize our possibilities. I slowly walked into the kitchen and stood. I wanted to feel his presence and hear his voice. Still no movement or sound. I walked to the letter and it was gone! I smiled and thought surely it resolved all things and he accepted it.

I felt good in an abnormal manner. It was not a complete goodness but one of hopefulness. I thought of Goldie and why he did not come back for me at the park. I called to ask Phoenix about him, but there was no answer in the office. The time had come to face off with Phoenix and return to work. I arrived for the start of dinnertime. I went into the office and no one was there. I began to look for Phoenix and Goldie. There were three customers at the bar and a few in the dining area. I saw the cellar door ajar and knew it was Phoenix stocking the bar. I went into the office to wait for him. Frankie entered and we stared in silence until he spoke. "Hi CC, glad you are here. We have a full house tonight for dinner. Are you ready to rock and roll?"

"Sure, where is Phoenix?"

"He called and said that there was confusion with the supply order and he went to the warehouse. He will be here later."

"Where is Goldie. I did not see him in the parking lot?"

"I thought he was out there, I will call and check on him later."

It was not long before the place was full and it kept us busy. I did not notice that Phoenix had not arrived until

SHE appeared. As she approached, my atmosphere was transformed. I did not know her name but from this night I would remember her face.

Her words were acute. "I have a reservation for Whitney."

As I looked for her name my atmosphere was shifting. I sensed her flagrant glare at me and that compelled me to try and make the connection. I lifted my head and our eyes connected. "Certainly, what time is your reservation?"

"I think he made it for 7:30pm." I saw her name for two at that time. Her presence was destructive as I escorted her to the table. I positioned both menus on the table and as we made eye contact there was an eerie vibe. I positioned both menus on the table and said "Enjoy your experience at Vinson Place." As I turned to walk away I heard her respond "I'm sure I will as I always have."

The next few hours were non-stop and I did not have time to ponder on Whitney. Besides, she sat alone, ordered two drinks and left without dinner at 8:15pm. I was relieved as she left with her unflattering demeanor. She was the distraught, attention-seeking-only-Phoenix-could-comfort patron. Of course I was relieved that she left dateless and to my satisfaction lonely. I had a fleeting thought of Phoenix and his whereabouts. It seemed as if it had been 24 hours without sight or sound of him. It was 1:30am when Frankie and I met in the office.

I silently hypothesized about Phoenix's whereabouts. Not wanting to appear concerned or alarmed I suggested that Frankie give me a ride home and to tell his brother that I was too tired to wait for him.

As I entered the home, that uncanny feeling arose. I quietly walked toward the bedroom and the bed was as I left it—with no Phoenix. It was not like him to be absent this long and never did we not speak for an entire day. How could he not try to have communication with me? Did he know about my hospitalization and did he care? I walked down to the basement and there he was ASLEEP. He seemed at peace and I dared not awaken him. I took a shower with my tears of fears and soon after was asleep.

I awoke to his voice talking on the phone. I could not hear all the words, I lay listening to delight and enjoyment as he spoke. His last words were, "Okay that is good, I will pick up the supplies and see you at the Place." I cautiously approached him as he was sitting on the sofa.

"Good morning, Honey. Would you like tea?" I asked.

"No thanks, I had a cup earlier." His voice was mildly mediocre. I thought to self—we must talk. I needed to access him with prudence and mostly love. I walked into the kitchen and started the tea kettle. I stood in the doorway not wanting to invade his space and with a pleading non-threatening tone said, "Baby I've missed you and want to talk with you so would you please have a cup of tea with me?" In the distance I could witness his unyielding and uncompromising resistance. With agitation he responded, "What would you like to talk about?"

At that point the kettle whistled and I thought, saved by the tea. I scurried and made hot tea for the both of us. As I walked toward him I felt imbalanced, but knew I had to convince him of our destiny. Knees trembling, I sat across from him as he gave a defiant stare. I wondered what had transpired with us for his detached coldness.

I began, "I love you and do not want to lose you. Tell me what is wrong so I can make it right. I am not at all angry with you, but I am highly confused with sadness. I was hopeful that if you read my letter, you would feel and know my love. If I could find the words to express how I adore, need and love you I am convinced that you would not desire to let me go...."

"STOP IT, STOP IT!" He rose and towered over me. "I simply do not love you anymore. I no longer love or desire to be in love with you. It is just that simple." Defenseless I could not speak for what seemed like an eternity. I sipped on tea for several moments. At last, I looked up at him and asked, "When and why did you stop loving me? One does not fall out of love for no apparent reason. What transpired that I know nothing about to compel you not to love me? Please, I am pleading with you to explain yourself and your actions."

At this point, rage encompassed my being. I began to scream angrily, crying profusely, trembling with maximum pain, hurt, betrayal, deceitfulness--the opposite of dedication, honesty, commitment, and love. He turned and walked away. I ran toward him and grabbed his arm, still demanding answers. "You answer me! When did this happen? You woke yesterday and for no apparent reason decided to cease loving me, cease wanting my love, cease wanting to share our lives, cease accomplishing and achieving with one another?"

He stood steadfast and dispassionately replied, "Yes, that is simply what happened. I awoke and no longer love nor want you. Sometimes in this life for no rhyme or reason one can just stop and no longer love or want the other person. I will give you a few weeks to leave and that is ample time. Basically, you arrived to a ready-made home with nothing. You may have all of your personal belongings when you leave."

I STOOD DEFENSELESS AND IN TOTAL SILENCE AND DISBELIEF!

He had become the monster that was dreadful and hid in the darkness of the closet. That monster had no name or face. That monster existed and no one else could envision or perceive it. I watched that monster as a child. I witnessed its destruction and havoc while it hid in the dark closet. That monster was now clear and present and it disabled my being. I was weak, not strong. I was not of tenacity but fragility. I was not confident but insecure. I was not valiant but cowardly. Somehow at this moment my inner-self recognized my flaws of acquiring love regardless of my relentless efforts. My inner-self was acquainted with the reality of this monster and would always try to persuade me to forfeit this journey of love, commitment and happiness.

I gathered my unvoiced, skeletal remains and I packed an overnight purse and left his home. As I walked directionless my only certainty was that I was uncertain of all reality.

THE FINAL FINALE OF MY LIFE HAS ARRIVED

Subsequently, I possessed an unforeseen blackout and my next consciousness was awakening in an abandoned section of the park. I had no recollection of how or why I was at the park. Nevertheless, it was the place where we had our first encounter.

Sitting on a bench in the darkness I questioned my worthiness to exist. I was frightened, angry, dismayed and with absolute loneliness. I ached to go home but had no home. Gazing at the stars, I was aching for light, but only crystal darkness appeared. I ached to live in this park that offered such serenity, and never to be seen or heard again. This outer-body experience was unsettling and uncontrollable. My thoughts ranged from melancholy to sinister. I appealed for the brilliant star to speak to me. I appealed for answers to the essential question—WHY? I tried to solicit all the compassion, love, respect, honesty, commitment, admiration, consideration and dedication to our lives together that lived in me before this betrayal of a heart break. I began to question the reality of the last seven years, seven months and six days. Was the beginning of our romance and the end of our love reality? I began to question all tangibles and intangibles of my life. Still there were so many unanswered questions. I looked above and screeched the words, "WHY ME DAMMIT? WHY ME?"

Hopelessly and helplessly I knelt whimpering for what seemed like hours until it felt as though I was all cried out. Brimming with numbness, doubt and aching for answers I began to aimlessly walk home. Oddly, I remained with the self-thought of us repairing our relationship. I continued to think that I must find the appropriate words and actions to convey that he is my life and I cannot live without him. Surely, if I can only make him recognize and accept that we belong together. There is no me without him and I will dedicate every waking moment to his happiness. Surely, I contributed to his abrupt change of emotions toward me. We have been very busy with the upcoming restaurant activities and I made very little time for us and I will rectify us.

I could recognize home at the end of the street. It seemed distant and remote. My legs grew weaker and my walk became lethargic. As I approached the door with key in hand, immense trepidation was clear and present. I paused and heard voices and laughter. Laughter I thought--this sound was bizarre and foreign. We had no laughter for an eternity and now it seemed the voices spoken were kind and the laughter was welcoming. I thought this was an opportune time for friends or family to visit. He needs this time for relaxation and heartwarming laughter. I dare not make my presence known at this time. I proceeded to the abandoned garage to sit until such time I would present myself.

As I passed an open kitchen window I heard a female voice sing to music. I noticed the back door was ajar. I soundlessly turned the knob and escaped to the basement. It was as if I was a burglar in my home. I maneuvered around the basement and in a daring attempt to distinguish and hear the voices I stood at the top of the basement stair. I would follow the sounds from room to room. It appeared as if they were having a party with only themselves. I could hear them singing love songs to one another. I needed to remain stalwart if I were to discover who this woman is. And it was definitely not Beverly.

I was engulfed in bewilderment, torment, anger and pain. It was as if this was a dreadful dream and any moment I would awaken from this awful nightmare.

Nonetheless, I had to be steadfast to get answers and closure.

Ultimately, it was time for the goodbye until next time. Their footsteps were approaching the back door. I positioned myself under the basement stairs with the door slightly ajar. My presence was concealed. Besides, with their jubilation that filled the atmosphere I was invisible as long as I remained silent.

Consequently, my silence gave way to an insufferable conclusion. I could hear them embracing and could feel their seemingly unwavering love for one another. They began to have an impulsive, passionate, committed, intense, critical and significant sexual love-making session (in the hallway for the back door exit.) As I listened to the moans and sighs of their sexual odyssey, I WAS MORTIFIED!

Undeniably, I was silenced to death. With every sigh and groan of ecstasy a slice of life left my body. I was reduced to a non entity, I had no sensation of a complete human being. In fact, I did not feel worthy of being considered an organism of any kind. I did not have a sensation that I was worthy of being soil from the Earth. My being became disconnected from all living creatures. I was experiencing an indescribable instant as I listened to their tenacious, indisputable and erotic love-making. Their undying commitment was sealed as both climaxed and professed their unyielding love for one another.

Approximately 20 to 30 minutes lapsed and I crept out the door and hid in the garage. I harvested enough self-pity to enter the home as if all was well.

I approached the front door noisily, as if I had tripped over something, so that he might not be unprepared for my entrance. As I put the key in the door my hand shook with tremendous trepidation. The danger zone was to capacity with the stench of unadulterated femininity and sex. I slammed the door pretending to be in pain from my fall and still it was an unnatural silence and stillness.

I stumbled to the kitchen, assuming he would be there in triumphant reflection and stillness. I cautiously continued throughout the house because of the deafening silence and no visible sign of him. I gave a theatrical performance with a water glass shattering and self inflicted cuts to my hand. I gave out a squeal of pain and ran to the bathroom.

As I passed the bedroom, I observed him sleeping there. I wondered why he had not awakened. I lay five to 10 minutes on the cold bathroom floor, swaying and crying for help, to no avail. He not once emerged from his comatose victory sleep.

I crawled across to the entrance of the bedroom and there he lay. I became enraged. I stood and scowled at him for several minutes. Then it happened—I CEASED TO EXIST—I WAS DECEASED!

I lost real time consciousness and revulsion of him engulfed my being. My emotional state was inexpressible as I stood over him, scrutinizing his blissful sleep.

It became essential for him to experience the existence which I was enduring. It became essential what must be done to this human vile maggot transformed hideous rodent.

I recalled a unique cutlery set that he purchased for me as a Valentine's Day gift. I would often complain of dull kitchen knives at home. Then a few years ago on V-Day I opened an incredible sharpened gold, black and red cutlery set. He had ordered it from the restaurant supplier—it was the kind that the chef's handled in the kitchen. The handle was red, and the blade was gold trimmed with black. He demonstrated the sharpness with slicing vegetables that I would toss in his direction. If the knife connected, the vegetable was practically shredded. It was an amazing spectacle. It was our dinette set centerpiece. It was enclosed in glass with a steel base sharpener. Our guests would often compliment my creation and thought it was ideal as a centerpiece surrounded with gold and black accessories. I was delighted with the gift and it was one of my treasures.

For the first time I stood admiring the exquisite enclosed glass and cutlery designed and thought it was elegant and delicate. Tears cascaded as I gravitated toward the set and with superb knife in hand I slowly walked toward "our" bedroom. How ironic the perfect gift given to me I will return to him on our last day of life together.

I reminisced early in our courtship pleading with him not to neglect, abuse, disregard or take advantage of my love. I explained in detail how heartbreak demolished my world and how difficult it was to reconstruct my life. I gave him the option multiple times to be honest with his motives. For two years I pleaded with him to depart the relationship if his intentions were not genuine in loving me and wanting us to spend our lives together. He always reassured me and demanded that we pledge our love and life to one another. Then we would make passionate love as our seal of the deal—each time I trusted and believed him.

Every inch and ounce of me trembled with fear until I became angry with myself for being petrified for realizing what I must do. I must terminate the earth of this unnatural debris, of this converted misrepresentation of a man. His moral compass is equivalent to that of all vermin. He must be extinguished from here and I must be the one to deliver him to his ultimate space.

I was at peace with my decision to KILL Phoenix. I was determined to plunge this exquisite large sharp knife into his heart and chest ensuring that he would not survive.

Standing over him I clenched the knife and aimed it toward his heart. Tears streaming uncontrollably, I raised the knife over my head and the unthinkable, inconceivable, unimaginable happened >>> >>

CONCLUSION TO FOLLOW
PART TWO (2)